Ms. Todd
Is Odd!

My Weird School #12

Ms. Todd Is Odd!

FERRIS PUBLIC LIBRARY

Dan Gutman

Pictures by
Jim Paillot

HarperTrophy®
An Imprint of HarperCollinsPublishers

Ms. Todd Is Odd!

Text copyright © 2006 by Dan Gutman

Illustrations copyright © 2006 by Jim Paillot

Library of Congress Cataloging-in-Publication Data is available.
ISBN-10: 0-06-082231-7 (pbk.) — ISBN-13: 978-0-06-082231-6 (pbk.)
ISBN-10: 0-06-082232-5 (lib. bdg.) — ISBN-13: 978-0-06-082232-3 (lib. bdg.)

❖

First Harper Trophy edition, 2006

Visit us on the World Wide Web!
www.harpercollinschildrens.com

To Emma

Contents

The Free Stuff Room

My name is A.J. and I hate school.

There's only one room in Ella Mentry School that I really like. It's the lost and found room!

The lost and found room is right near the office. It is the coolest room in the history of the world because there is

1

lots of free stuff in there. Me and my friends Michael and Ryan call it "the free stuff room." You can get just about anything you want, and you don't even have to pay for it. So if I feel like getting a new baseball cap or a pair of sunglasses, I don't have to go to a store. I just go to the free stuff room at school. It's awesome!

So this one morning the bus got to school a little early, and I went to kill some time in the free stuff room. I saw a really cool black T-shirt with a lightning bolt across the back. It was way cooler than the shirt I was wearing, so I took my shirt off and put the cool one on. It fit perfectly. I stuffed my old, boring shirt in my backpack.

It was almost time to pledge the allegiance, so I went to class. The kids were putting their backpacks and lunch boxes in their cubbies. Our teacher, Miss Daisy, wasn't there yet. That was weird. She usually gets to school before any of us.

"Where's Miss Daisy?" asked Neil, who everybody calls "the nude kid." He actually wears clothes, but we call him "the nude kid" anyway. It's a long story.

"Maybe she got lost," Michael said.

Suddenly the door opened. We all looked up. But it wasn't Miss Daisy.

It was Andrea Young, this really

annoying little Miss Perfect girl with curly brown hair who I hate. She's such a nerd. She even keeps a dictionary on her desk in case she ever has to look up a word.

"Where *were* you, Andrea?" asked her equally annoying crybaby friend, Emily. "I was worried that you were sick. There's something going around, you know."

"I wasn't sick," Andrea said. "I had to go to Mr. Klutz's office."

"Oooooh!" we all went.

Mr. Klutz is the principal of the school. He also has no hair. Kids get sent to his office when they do something bad.

"Did you do something bad?" asked

Emily, all concerned.

"Of course not!" Andrea said. "Mr. Klutz called me in to say I'm going to be in the gifted and talented program!"

Oh man! That figured. The gifted and talented program is for dorks, dweebs, nerds, and know-it-alls like Andrea who are perfect in every way. We all took some dumb test a few weeks ago, and Andrea probably got the best score in the whole school.

"Isn't that fabulous?" Andrea said. "I'm gifted and talented!"

"What's your talent?" I asked her. "Being annoying?"

Some of the kids laughed. Andrea gave

me one of her mean looks.

"I like your shirt, Arlo," she said. "Where did you get it?"

"None of your beeswax," I told her. I hate when Andrea calls me by my real name.

"Oh yeah?" she said. "Well, I think it *is* my beeswax, because that's *my* shirt!"

What?!

"That shirt fell out of my backpack last week," Andrea said. "I was wondering where it was."

Everybody started giggling. I thought I was gonna die. I was wearing a girl's shirt! Not only was I wearing a girl's shirt, but it was *Andrea*'s shirt! Her girl

cooties were crawling all over me! It was disgusting. I thought I was gonna throw up.

"Oooooh!" Ryan said. "A.J. is wearing

Andrea's shirt. They must be in *love*!"

"When are you gonna get married?" asked Michael.

If those guys weren't my best friends, I would hate them.

Something Going Around

I ripped the T-shirt off like it was on fire and threw it at Andrea.

"Ewwww, it's disgusting!" she said. "I'll never wear this shirt again! It has A.J.'s boy cooties all over it. I'll have to burn—"

Andrea never got the chance to finish her sentence, because at that very second

Mr. Klutz came in with his bald head. He was wearing a black T-shirt that said TEAM on it.

"What's going on in here?" Mr. Klutz asked.

I grabbed my old shirt out of my backpack and quickly put it on.

"A.J. thinks the classroom is a dressing room," Andrea said.

What is her problem? Why can't a giant box full of T-shirts fall on her head?

"I just got a call from Miss Daisy," Mr. Klutz told us. "She's not feeling well today. So you'll have Ms. Todd as your substitute teacher. She'll be here any minute."

Mr. Klutz said he would go to the office to greet Ms. Todd. He told us to be on our best behavior while he was gone. So as soon as Mr. Klutz left the room, me and Michael and Ryan got up and shook our butts at the class. Most of the kids laughed.

"I hope Ms. Todd is nice," said Andrea. Girls always want everybody to be nice.

"I hope Miss Daisy is going to be all right," said Emily. She looked all worried, like she was going to cry. That girl will cry about any old thing. She's weird.

"We should make Miss Daisy a get-well card," said one of the other girls.

Miss Daisy better get well soon, because I hate substitute teachers. They always make us learn stuff. Miss Daisy never makes us learn anything, because she doesn't *know* anything. She is the only grown-up who can't read, write, or do arithmetic. In fact, sometimes we have to teach *her* stuff! She is the dumbest teacher in the history of the world.

Miss Daisy asked us once not to tell Mr. Klutz how dumb she is. She's afraid she'll get fired. I hoped Ms. Todd would be as dumb as Miss Daisy.

"You know," Ryan said, "Miss Daisy didn't look sick yesterday."

"Maybe she's not sick at all," said Michael.

"Yeah," I said, "maybe she's faking it so she can stay home and lie on her couch eating bonbons."

Bonbons are these chocolate treats Miss Daisy loves. She told us that whenever she is stressed out, she lies on her couch and eats bonbons until she feels better.

"Do you think Mr. Klutz found out that Miss Daisy can't read or write or do arithmetic?" asked Neil the nude kid. "So he fired—"

Neil the nude kid never got the chance to finish his sentence, because the door opened again and Mr. Klutz came in. He was with some lady.

"Boys and girls," said Mr. Klutz, "this is Ms. Todd. She'll be the substitute for Miss Daisy."

We all looked at Ms. Todd. Ms. Todd looked at us. I looked at Andrea. Ryan and Michael looked at me. Everybody was looking at everybody else without saying anything because it was the most amazing thing in the history of the world.

Ms. Todd looked like Andrea!

It's true! She was tall just like Andrea. She was skinny just like Andrea. She even had curly hair just like Andrea. It was like there were *two* of them! It was like a horror movie!

"She's pretty," whispered Andrea.

"Pretty ugly," I whispered.

Ms. Todd was wearing a TEAM T-shirt just like Mr. Klutz.

"Why are you both wearing T-shirts that say TEAM?" asked Ryan.

"TEAM is our new motto at Ella Mentry School," said Mr. Klutz. "It stands for

'Together Everyone Achieves More.'" Mr. Klutz loves initials.

"What's a motto?" asked Michael.

"Nothing," said Mr. Klutz. "What's a motto with you?"

Mr. Klutz laughed even though he didn't say anything funny. He's nuts.

Ms. Todd waved and smiled a big smiley face just like Andrea. She looked really young. Mr. Klutz said that Ms. Todd was a brand-new teacher and told us to be extra nice to her. Then he left.

"Hello!" said Ms. Todd, all cheery.

Well, at least she talked like a regular person. Our bus driver, Mrs. Kormel, speaks in a secret language. Instead of saying "hello" like everybody else, she says, "Bingle boo." Mrs. Kormel is not normal.

"Hi, Ms. Todd," said little Miss Gifted and Talented. "My name is Andrea. I love the shoes you're wearing."

Andrea wasn't wasting any time before starting in with her brownnosing. I hate her.

"Why, thank you!" exclaimed Ms. Todd. "That's very sweet of you to say. I like your shoes too, Andrea."

Andrea totally didn't know how you're supposed to treat subs. You're supposed to torture them! That's the first rule of being a kid. My friend Billy who lives around the corner told me that whenever a sub turns her back, his whole class starts coughing* for no reason. He said it drives the sub crazy.

Ms. Todd went to write her name on the board. As soon as she turned around and wrote *MS.*, I started coughing for no reason.

Ms. Todd turned around and looked at the class. But I stopped coughing before she saw me.

*Can I just say something here? Isn't c-o-u-g-h a dumb way to spell "cough"? It should be k-o-f-f. Whoever wrote the dictionary is a dumbhead.

Ms. Todd faced the board again and wrote the letter *T.* I started coughing again. Ryan started coughing too.

Ms. Todd turned around and looked at the class. Me and Ryan stopped coughing before she saw us.

Ms. Todd faced the board again and wrote the letter *O.* Me and Ryan started coughing again.

Ms. Todd turned around real fast and looked at the class. Me and Ryan stopped coughing just in time.

Ms. Todd faced the board again and wrote the letter *D.* Me and Ryan started coughing again.

Ms. Todd started writing another letter

D, but in the middle of it, she turned around really fast and looked at us. Me and Ryan were still coughing.

Uh-oh. Me and Ryan were in trouble.

"What's your name?" Ms. Todd asked me.

Everybody looked at me. I didn't know

what to say. I didn't know what to do. I had to think fast.

That's when I got the greatest idea in the history of the world. If I didn't tell Ms. Todd my real name, I wouldn't get in trouble!

"My name is Ryan," I said.

"And how about you?" Ms. Todd asked Ryan. "What's your name?"

"My name is A.J.," said Ryan.

Ms. Todd took a piece of paper from Miss Daisy's desk and wrote something on it.

"Well," she said, "Ryan and A.J. are going to be in trouble."

I guess my idea wasn't so great after all.

If You Don't Have Something Nice to Say, Say Something Mean

3

Even after Ms. Todd wrote my name on her piece of paper, she still had on a big smiley face. It must hurt to smile so much. My friend Billy who lives around the corner told me that if you keep smiling too long, your face muscles get frozen like that forever.

Ms. Todd told us all to sit in a big circle on the floor.

"Let's go around the room and say something nice about the person sitting across from us," she said. "This will help me learn your names and get to know you better."

"Annette is a really
good soccer player," said
this girl named Lindsay.

"Lindsay knows everything
about horses," said Annette.

"Michael is really good at sports," said
Ryan.

"Ryan is a really good eater," said
Michael. "He will even eat stuff that isn't
food."

25

I looked to see who was sitting across from me. Ugh. It was Andrea! I hoped that I wouldn't get called on.

"Your turn, Andrea," said Ms. Todd.

Andrea looked at me for a long time.

"A.J. is really good at picking out clothes," she finally said. Then she stuck her tongue out at me when Ms. Todd wasn't looking.

"Wait a minute," Ms. Todd said to me. "I thought you said your name was Ryan."

"I'm Ryan," said Ryan.

"He's a liar," said Andrea. "His name is A.J. That stands for Arlo Jervis."

Ms. Todd went over to the desk and

wrote something else down on that piece of paper of hers. Then she came back to the circle.

"A.J., it's your turn. Can you tell the class something nice about Andrea?"

I looked at Andrea for a long time. There wasn't anything nice about her.

"It would be nice if an elephant fell on her head," I said.

"That's not nice, A.J.!" said Ms. Todd.

"It's the truth," I said. "I hate her."

"I hate you right back!" said Andrea.

"I hate you right back back!" I said.

"I hate you right back back back!" Andrea said.

We went on like that for a while.

"A.J.," Ms. Todd said. "You were supposed to say something *nice* about Andrea. Don't you think she has nice hair?"

"No."

"Doesn't she have nice clothes?"

"No."

"Then why did you steal my shirt?" Andrea asked.

"I didn't steal it!" I said.

"Did too!"

"Did not!"

We went on like that for a while until Ms. Todd told me I had to write a note to Andrea telling her I was sorry.

So this is what I wrote:

Dear Andrea,
I'm sorry I hate you.
A.J.

"Let's try to work together as a T-E-A-M," said Ms. Todd. "As you know, Together Everyone Achieves More. So we need cooperation. Do you know what 'cooperation' means?"

"Isn't that a company?" asked Emily.

"That's 'corporation,' dumbhead," I said.

"You're mean!" said Emily. She looked like she was going to cry. What is her problem?

"Don't say 'dumbhead,'" Ms. Todd told me as she wrote something else on that piece of paper of hers. "Say *smart* head.

Calling somebody a dumbhead might hurt their feelings."

"I know," I said. "That's why I did it."

Ms. Todd thinks she knows everything. Just like Andrea. I'll bet that when she was a kid, Ms. Todd was in the gifted and talented program.

My Head Almost Exploded

4

"Is everybody ready to learn?" asked Ms. Todd.

"Yes!" yelled all the girls.

"No!" yelled all the boys.

"All right!" yelled Ms. Todd.

Ms. Todd is one of those teachers who is full of excitement all the time. She never sits down. She runs around for no reason, clapping her hands, like my mom does when she drinks too much coffee. If you ask me, Ms. Todd should calm down. She's like one of those windup toy monkeys that plays the drums. Maybe after she has been a teacher for a few years, she'll become normal and not so excited about teaching kids stuff anymore.

"Let's start with reading!" said Ms. Todd, smiling her smiley face and clapping her hands and running around the class for no reason.

"I love to read," said Andrea, who loves everything. "I'm going to write a children's book someday, and the main character will be named Andrea. Then I'll be famous!"

"I *love* reading children's books," said Ms. Todd. "I read them all the time!"

"Even when you're sleeping?" asked Ryan.

"Even when you're driving?" asked Michael.

"Even when you're in the shower?" I asked.

"Well, no, not then," Ms. Todd said.

"So why did you say you read them all the time?" asked Michael.

"It's just an expression," said Ms. Todd.

"Is an expression the same thing as lying?" I asked.

Ms. Todd stopped smiling her smiley face and wrote something down on that piece of paper again. I wished she would stop doing that.

Next she read to us for about a million hundred hours. She read a story about a girl and her dog. It was the most boring story in the history of the world. Nothing ever happened in that dumb story. I almost fell asleep, but then the girl's dog got hit by a car and the story got interesting. Some of the girls were crying. What a bunch of babies!

After the dog died, Ms. Todd stopped reading the story. She taught us about the solar system and the explorers and Australia and Helen Keller and lots of other stuff, too. She taught us so much stuff that I had a headache.

My friend Billy who lives around the corner told me that if you learn too much stuff too fast, your head will explode. I'm going to have to forget some of the old stuff I learned to make room for all the new stuff Ms. Todd taught us. I don't want my head to explode.

Finally the lunch bell rang, and Ms. Todd had to stop teaching us stuff. Michael was the line leader as we walked to the vomitorium to eat.

"Ms. Todd is a horrible teacher," I said. "All she does is make us learn stuff."

"I miss Miss Daisy," Ryan said. "She never taught us anything."

"I miss miss Miss Daisy," said Michael.

"I miss miss miss Miss Daisy," I said.

We went on like that for a while until the queen of the gifted and talented butted in.

"You boys are dumbheads," said Andrea. "Learning new things is fun and makes us better people."

"Can you possibly be any more boring?" I asked her.

Andrea is just like Ms. Todd. They look alike. They talk alike. They smile alike. They're both perfect all the time. It's like they are the same person. It's uncanny.[**]

I think I hate both of them.

[**]That means it's not like a can, because "un" means "not" and "canny" means "like a can."

Indoor Recess Is No Fun at All

It was Spaghetti and Meatballs Day in the vomitorium, but I always bring lunch from home. I wouldn't eat the school lunch if I was living in Antarctica and starving.

Ryan gave me his Pop-Tart. I gave him my grapes because I don't like to eat food with pits in it. Ryan will eat anything.

One time he ate a piece of a seat cushion.

We all agreed that Ms. Todd is way too happy.

"Nobody is that happy," said Michael.

"People who are happy all the time are weird," I said.

"Did you notice that Ms. Todd smiles all the time?" asked Ryan. "She probably smiles when she gets a paper cut or stubs her—"

He never had the chance to finish his sentence, because at that second Mr. Klutz's voice came over the loudspeaker.

"I have an announcement to make," said Mr. Klutz. "It is raining out, so we will have indoor recess today. After lunch please return to your classrooms."

"Boooooo!" everybody hollered, even the girls.

Bummer in the summer! I hate indoor recess. Recess is the only fun part of the day, and now we would have to stay in the class with that learning lunatic Ms. Todd. After we cleared off the lunch table, me and Ryan and Michael had a race to see who could walk back to our classroom the slowest. I won.

Ms. Todd was in there, all excited and clapping her hands and running around the class for no reason.

"Do we have to learn more stuff now?" Ryan asked.

"Of course not!" said Ms. Todd. "This is recess. Let's play a game!"

"Can we play cops and robbers?" Michael asked. "I call robbers!"

"That game sounds dangerous," said Ms. Todd. "How about another game?"

"Let's play army," said Ryan. "Boys against girls. Bang, bang! You're dead!"

"Can anybody think of a game that

doesn't involve shooting?" asked Ms. Todd.

"We could play NASCAR," I suggested. "There's no shooting in NASCAR."

"I never heard of that game, A.J.," said Ms. Todd. "How do you play NASCAR?"

"We run around in circles," I told her, "and every few laps we smash into each other."

"That sounds quite violent," said Ms. Todd.

"Yeah, and it's cool, too," I told her.

I knew that if we didn't come up with something fast, one of the girls would suggest square dancing or some corny game.

"I know a good game we can play," I

suggested. "It's called see who can hit the softest."

"Now that doesn't sound violent," said Ms. Todd. "How do you play?"

I told Neil the nude kid to stand up and see how softly he could hit me. He barely tapped my arm.

"That's pretty soft," I told Neil the nude kid. "Now it's my turn."

I made a fist with my hand and punched Neil the nude kid really hard on the arm.

"Owwwwwwwww!" cried Neil the nude kid.

"Oops," I said. "I lose!"

It was hilarious. Neil the nude kid will fall for anything. All the boys laughed. Well, all the boys except for Neil the nude kid. He just rubbed his arm.

"That's a terrible game, A.J.!" shouted Ms. Todd. She wrote something down on her piece of paper.

Ms. Todd wasn't smiling for a change. She told Neil the nude kid to go see Mrs. Cooney, the school nurse. Then she told me to go to Mr. Klutz's office.

"What did I do?" I asked. "I was just playing see who can hit the softest."

"Go to Mr. Klutz's office!" yelled Ms. Todd. "Now!"

Good News?

Mr. Klutz's office is really cool. He has a snowboarding poster on the wall and a punching bag in the corner with a face painted on it.

I wasn't too worried. The last time I got sent to the principal's office for being bad, Mr. Klutz gave me a candy bar. It was the greatest day of my life.

When I opened his door, Mr. Klutz
wasn't sitting at his desk like a normal
principal. He was hanging upside down
from a bar attached to the ceiling. He
had on boots that were attached to the

bar. He says that when the blood rushes to his head, it helps him think.

Mr. Klutz is nuts.

"Come in, A.J.," he said as he pulled himself out of the boots and fell into his chair.

"I'm sorry I punched Neil the nude kid," I said. "I won't do it again."

"I understand, A.J.," Mr. Klutz said. "I was a boy once."

"Just once?" I asked. "I'm a boy *all* the time."

Mr. Klutz laughed even though I didn't say anything funny.

"A.J., I have some good news for you," Mr. Klutz said.

"You're going to give me a candy bar?" I guessed.

"Oh, better than that," Mr. Klutz said. "I'm happy to inform you that you have been selected for the gifted and talented program!"

"What?!"

"Remember that test the whole school took a few weeks ago?" he said. "Well, you scored very high. We think you are gifted and talented. Congratulations, A.J.!"

Gifted and talented? I don't

want to be gifted and talented! Dorks and dweebs like Andrea are gifted and talented. Not cool kids like me! I just wanted to be normal. I just wanted a candy bar.

"There must have been a mistake," I said. "Can I take the test again? I'm sure I'll do a lot worse."

Mr. Klutz laughed again, even though I didn't say anything funny.

"I'm sure you're anxious to get back to class and tell everyone the good news," he said.

No I wasn't. If the kids in class found out I was gifted and talented, they'd think I was a dork like Andrea.

What could I do? As I walked down the hall back to class, I thought of my options:

1. I could change my name and wear a fake nose and glasses so nobody would know who I was.
2. I could keep a paper bag over my head for the rest of my life.
3. I could go live with the penguins in Antarctica. Penguins are cool.
4. I could just keep my mouth shut and hope nobody ever found out I was gifted and talented.

"What did Mr. Klutz do to you?" Michael whispered as soon as I got back to class. "Did he kick you out of school?"

No way I was going to tell Michael I was gifted and talented.

"He tortured me," I told Michael. "He put me in a machine that spun me around until I threw up. Then he made me shine his head with a rag. Then he made me eat smelly cheese. Then he made me listen to some of his old music from the 1980s. It was horrible. I thought I was gonna die."

"Cool!" Ryan said.

Circle of Friends

"I love math!" Ms. Todd said after recess, smiling her smiley face and clapping her hands and running around the class for no reason. Where does she get all the energy?

"I love math too!" said Andrea.

"If you had ten chocolate ice cream cones," said Ms. Todd, "and you gave me five of them, how many chocolate ice-cream cones would you have left? A.J.?"

"None," I said. "Because I would throw them all in the garbage. I like mint chip ice cream."

Ms. Todd wrote something on her piece of paper. Then she made us do addition and subtraction for about a million hundred hours. The worst part was, she made me be study buddies with Andrea. It was horrible.

"Isn't math fun, A.J.?" asked Andrea.

"Oh yes," I said, "and so is being attacked by an angry gorilla."

Ms. Todd is just like Andrea. She loves school. She loves reading. She loves math. She loves *everything*. Ms. Todd and Andrea are like two peas in an iPod.

"Let's draw pictures!" Ms. Todd said after math was over. "I love drawing pictures!"

"Do you hate *anything*?" I asked Ms. Todd.

She thought about it for a minute.

"I hate people who hate," Ms. Todd finally said.

"I hate people who hate people who hate," said Ryan.

"I hate people who hate people who hate people who hate," said Michael.

"I hate people who—"

I never got the chance to finish my sentence because Ms. Todd told us to be quiet and start drawing.

Andrea drew a picture of her face with a butterfly on her nose. Emily drew a picture of flowers from all different countries holding hands with each other. (What a dumbhead! Flowers don't even *have* hands.) I drew a picture of some alien spaceships attacking a school with laser beams. Then I drew this cool action figure named Striker Smith flying in on a jet plane and shooting the aliens until they were all dead. It was awesome.

"That's quite violent, A.J.," Ms. Todd said when she walked around the class, looking at our pictures. Then she wrote something down on that dumb piece of paper of hers.

What was her problem? Every time I said anything, she wrote something down on that dumb piece of paper. I couldn't take it anymore.

"What are you writing on that piece of paper?" I asked.

"Oh, you'll find out," Ms. Todd said.

After we finished our pictures, Ms. Todd said the rain had stopped so we could go out to the playground to burn off some energy.

"Can we play tag?" I asked. "Please please please please please?"

"Tag can be a very violent game," Ms. Todd said. "Let's play circle of friends instead!"

"What's that?"

"It's a lot like tag," Ms. Todd explained, "except that when you tag people, they don't become *it*. They become your new friends. The object of the game is to see how many friends you can make."

If you asked me, that sounded like the dumbest game in the history of the world.

Emily got to go first. She tagged Andrea. Now Andrea was in her circle of friends. Andrea tried to tag me, but I play peewee football, so I knew how to get away from her. Nah-nah-nah boo-boo on her!

The only problem was that Ryan and Michael play peewee football too. They thought it would be funny to sneak up from behind and tackle me. So that's what they did. When I was on the ground, Andrea ran over and tagged me.

"Oooooh!" Ryan said. "A.J. is in Andrea's circle of friends. They must be in *love*!"

"When are you gonna get married?" asked Michael.

I wanted to punch them, but I didn't want Ms. Todd to write anything else down on that dumb piece of paper.

"See?" said Ms. Todd. "You can have fun

without being competitive!"

We played that dumb circle of friends game for about a million hundred hours. It was horrible. I thought I was gonna die.

Luckily Emily fell down and started crying as always, so we had to stop playing. Ms. Todd let us go back inside. We still had some time left before the dismissal bell was going to ring.

"Let's play musical chairs!" I suggested.

Musical chairs is awesome. Everybody walks around a bunch of chairs and when the music stops, you fight over the chairs. It's a cool game because you get to knock other kids on their butts.

"Musical chairs is very competitive," Ms. Todd said. "Whenever there is a winner, there has to be a loser, and that's sad. Competition causes bad feelings."

Can she possibly be more boring?

"I have an idea," I said. "Let's have a contest to see who can be the least competitive! The winning team could get a trophy or something that says they were less competitive than anybody else."

"I don't think you quite understand the idea of not competing," said Ms. Todd. Then she wrote something on her dumb piece of paper again.

I was afraid that Ms. Todd was going

to come up with some other weird non-violent game for us to play. But finally the bell rang, and we were allowed to get out of jail. I mean, we were allowed to go home.

I think that was the worst day of my life. The only good thing about it was that my head didn't explode.

Getting the Goods on Ms. Todd

I couldn't wait to get to school the next day. Yes, you heard that right! I *wanted* to go to school for the first time in history. That was because weird Ms. Todd would be gone and good old Miss Daisy would be back. Mom said I could ride my bike to school so I wouldn't have to

wait for the bus. Mrs. Kormel, the bus driver, gets lost all the time. She's not normal.

It was Flag Day, so we all wore red, white, and blue to school. There were flags of all different countries all over the place. When I walked in the class, Miss Daisy wasn't there yet. But Andrea was sitting there with this pruny mean face on and her arms folded in front of her like an *x*.

"What's eating you?" I asked her. "Did somebody steal your dictionary?"

"You *know* why I'm mad, A.J.," she said.

"No I don't."

"Yes you do."

We went back and forth like that for a while, until Andrea finally said why she was mad.

"I found out that *you're* gifted and talented," she whispered. "It's not fair!"

"Who told you?" I asked.

"My mother," Andrea said. "She's vice president of the PTA. She knows everything."

"Well, I'm not telling anyone," I whispered. "I don't want the guys to know I'm a gifted and talented dork like you."

"I'm not telling anyone either," Andrea said. "I want to be the only one in the class who's gifted and talented."

"Agreed," I said. "It will be our secret."

The only problem was that Ryan was hiding under his desk listening to us the whole time.

"Oooooh!" Ryan said. "A.J. and Andrea are both gifted and talented. They must be in *love*! When are you gonna get—"

Ryan never got the chance to finish his sentence because at that very second, guess who walked into the door?

Nobody! It would be dumb to walk into a door. But guess who walked into the doorway?

Ms. Todd!

Oh no! The Andrea clone was *back*. It was like a horror movie!

"Miss Daisy is still sick," Ms. Todd said. "There must be something going around. So I'll be your teacher again today."

She didn't look all that happy about it. She wasn't nearly as smiley as she was the day before. "Open up your math books."

Ugh! We had to do reading and writing and math all morning. I thought my head was going to explode. Then Ms. Todd forced us to play more of her dumb games where nobody wins or loses. What's the point of playing? I thought I was gonna die. I couldn't wait for lunchtime.

"I miss Miss Daisy," Ryan said as soon as we sat down in the vomitorium.

"I miss miss Miss Daisy," said Michael. "Ms. Todd is weird."

"Do you notice that every time I say anything, she writes something down on her piece of paper?" I asked. "What's up with that?"

"Subs have to write a report about what happens in class," Andrea said. "You're going to be in big trouble when Miss Daisy gets back and reads Ms. Todd's report."

"All Ms. Todd ever does is teach stuff," said Ryan. "She's like a robot teacher."

"Hey, maybe Ms. Todd isn't a teacher at all," I said. "Did you ever think of that?"

"What do you mean?" asked Emily.

"Maybe she's a robot in the body of a human, and she was sent here to take over the Earth," I said. "I saw that in a movie once."

"Stop trying to scare Emily," Andrea said.

"I'll bet that robot Ms. Todd murdered Miss Daisy so she could take over her job," Michael said. "Subs do that all the time, you know."

"Yeah," I said, "after the robot subs murder all the human teachers, they'll probably create a race of robot zombie clones to brainwash kids and take over the world."

"If Ms. Todd finds out we know," Ryan said, "she might murder one of us to keep us quiet."

"We've got to *do* something!" said Emily, and she went running out of the vomitorium.

Emily is weird.

"Maybe we should call the police," Ryan suggested. "They could arrest Ms. Todd."

"We need to find some evidence first," said Michael, "so we can get the goods on her."

"What goods?" I asked.

"I don't know," Michael said. "But you always have to get the goods on criminals."

Michael's dad is a policeman, so he knows all about crime and murder and stuff.

After lunch we headed back to class. Me and Ryan and Michael tiptoed around the hallway pretending to be detectives so we could get the goods on Ms. Todd. It was cool.

"If there *has* been a murder," Michael told us when we got to our classroom, "there has to be a murder weapon. You guys look around for one. I'll see if I can find a few strands of Ms. Todd's hair."

"Why do you want her hair?" I asked.

"So my dad can do a DNA test on it," Michael said. "Once we get her hair, we'll have the goods on her and we can throw her in the slammer."

I still didn't know why we needed Ms. Todd's hair. I didn't know what a slammer or DNA were either. But I didn't say anything because I figured gifted and talented kids like me should know stuff like that.

No one was back from lunch yet. Ms. Todd was probably still in the teachers' lounge. That's a room where teachers sit around in hot tubs all day. So me and Ryan looked around the classroom for murder weapons. A piece of chalk? A flag? The blackboard eraser? It would be really hard to murder somebody with an eraser.

"What if you forced somebody to *eat* the eraser?" asked Ryan. He is always thinking about eating stuff that is not food. Ryan is weird.

"Did you find the murder weapon yet?" Michael asked us.

"No," I said. "Did you find a strand of Ms. Todd's hair?"

"No," he said.

"So what do we do now?" asked Ryan.

"We'll have to question Ms. Todd," Michael told us. "We need to find out where she was two days ago, the last time Miss Daisy was seen alive."

We had to stop snooping around because Ms. Todd and the kids from our class came in. She told us all to sit down and then she started talking about Flag Day. Some countries have really dumb flags.[***] I think she made some of them up.

"Does anyone have any questions?" Ms. Todd finally asked.

"I do," I said. "Where were you two days ago?"

[***]Did you know that the flag of Barbados has a picture of a pitchfork on it? That's weird.

"I beg your pardon?" asked Ms. Todd.

"You heard me," I said. "Where were you two days ago?"

"What does that have to do with Flag Day?" she asked.

"Don't want to answer, eh?" I said. "Then you must be guilty."

"Guilty of what?" Ms. Todd said. "It's none of your business where I was two days ago."

"If you won't answer the questions," I said, "we're going to need your hair."

"My hair?" asked Ms. Todd. "Why?"

"We need to run a DNA test so we can get the goods on you and throw you in the slammer."

I took my scissors out of my pencil box.

"Don't be ridiculous," said Ms. Todd.

"Give me your DNA," I insisted, getting up from my desk.

"No!" said Ms. Todd, backing away from me.

"She's getting away!" yelled Michael.

So I did the only thing I could do. I started chasing Ms. Todd around the classroom.

"A.J. is going crazy!" shouted Andrea.

"We've got to do something!" shouted Emily.

"Never run with scissors!" yelled Ms. Todd.

"Get her, Ryan!" shouted Michael, and

the three of us chased Ms. Todd around the classroom. It was a real Kodak moment.

"You're under arrest for the murder of Miss Daisy!" Ryan yelled.

"You kids are crazy!" yelled Ms. Todd.

"Admit it!" I yelled. "You're a killer robot clone! You want to take over the world!"

"Help!" yelled Ms. Todd.

"You have the right to remain silent," Michael said. "Anything you say will be used against you."

"You're a bunch of little monsters!" Ms. Todd yelled. "I quit! I don't want to be a teacher anymore!"

Then she ran out the door. It was cool.

You should have been there.

Ms. Todd is odd.

The Truth About Ms. Todd

After Ms. Todd ran away, none of us said anything for a million hundred seconds. I had never heard of a sub who freaked out and went nuts before. And we got to see it live and in person.

But now that killer robot clone was on the loose. If we chased her out of school and around the parking lot, though, we'd be in big trouble.

That's when I thought of something. Ms. Todd forgot to take that piece of paper she was always writing on! I could grab it and hide it so nobody would ever know about all the bad stuff I did while we had a sub.

What a genius idea. No wonder I'm gifted and talented.

I went over to Miss Daisy's desk.

"You better leave that paper alone, A.J.," said Andrea.

"Mind your own beeswax, Andrea."

I found the piece of paper Ms. Todd had been writing on.

"You're going to be in big trouble, A.J.,"
said Andrea.

I picked up the piece of paper.

"I'm telling, A.J.," said Andrea.

I looked at the piece of paper.

All the other kids got out of their seats
and gathered around me. Even Andrea.

This is what the piece of paper said. . . .

I'm not going to tell you.

Okay, okay, I'll tell you. This is what it said:

TITLE: My Wacky School

By Arlene Todd

CHARACTERS: Boy who hates school. Smart girl.

BEGINNING: Sub arrives. Kids cough when she turns her back. Kids switch names to confuse sub. Kids tease each other. Kids are annoying.

MIDDLE: Kids call each other "dumb-head." Teacher says she reads all the time. See who can hit the softest. Kid would throw chocolate cones away because he likes mint chip. Picture of alien spaceships attacking school. Contest to see who can be the least competitive. Sub isn't sure she can make it through the day.

ENDING:

"Hey," I said, "this isn't a report for Miss Daisy!"

"Of course not, dumbhead!" said Andrea. "Ms. Todd was writing a children's book! She was going to call it *My Wacky School*! And it was going to be about our class! We could have been famous! You messed it up, A.J. Now, thanks to you, everything is ruined."

"So is your face," I said.

Well, maybe Ms. Todd wasn't a robot after all. But she was a terrible teacher. And she murdered Miss Daisy, who was nice.

I wouldn't want to be in some dumb children's book anyway.

Our Best Behavior

After Ms. Todd freaked out and ran away, we all agreed not to tell anyone what happened. Even Andrea. Our lips were sealed. (But not with glue. That would have been weird.) We decided to be on our best behavior so nobody would know what we did.

We were all sitting there with our hands folded (but not like a piece of paper) when Mr. Klutz rushed in with his bald head. He was wearing a jacket and tie.

"I have an important meeting to get to," he said. "What's going on in here? What did you kids do to Ms. Todd? I've never seen anyone run through the parking lot so fast."

"We didn't do anything," said Ryan.

"She just freaked out," said Michael. "We had nothing to do with it."

I looked over at Andrea to make sure she wasn't going to blab.

"What happened, A.J.?" demanded Mr.

Klutz. "Something tells me *you* had something to do with this."

I didn't know what to say. I didn't know what to do. I had to think fast.

"I think maybe Ms. Todd decided to enter the Olympics," I said. "She is a really fast runner, and she was going to run a few laps around the—"

But I never had the chance to finish my sentence. Because at that moment, the most amazing thing in the history of the world happened. The door opened.

Well, actually that wasn't the amazing part, because doors open all the time. The amazing part was who walked in the door.

Well, actually nobody walked *in* the door. If somebody walked in the door, it would hurt. You walk in a door-*way*.

Anyway, the most amazing thing in the history of the world was the person who walked in the doorway.

It was Miss Daisy!

Playing Dumb

"Miss Daisy!" we all shouted. "You're not dead!"

"Of course I'm not dead," she said, blowing her nose. "I had the sniffles. There's something going around, you know."

Even though Miss Daisy was sick, we all got up and hugged her. I was glad she was back so we could stop learning stuff.

"Where did Ms. Todd go?" asked Emily, like she was all worried.

"I have no idea," said Miss Daisy. "Somebody in the office said she freaked out. What did you kids do to her?"

"Nothing!" we all lied.

"It was like she just disappeared," I said. "We didn't chase her with scissors or anything."

"Ms. Todd never even said good-bye," said Andrea. "That wasn't very nice."

"I think she went to try out for the Olympics," said Michael.

"Ms. Todd was a terrible teacher," said

Ryan. "All she wanted to do was teach us stuff."

"It must have been horrible!" said Miss Daisy.

Suddenly I figured it all out. It was like in the cartoons when a lightbulb appears on top of somebody's head so you know they had a great idea. Well, I had a great idea. I finally figured out what *really* happened.

It wasn't that Ms. Todd murdered Miss Daisy. It was that Miss Daisy murdered Ms. Todd!

Now it all made sense. Everything fit together. Miss Daisy probably suspected that Ms. Todd knew a lot of stuff to teach

us. She was afraid that Ms. Todd knew so much stuff that Mr. Klutz might hire her to take over Miss Daisy's job. So Miss Daisy murdered Ms. Todd. She was just playing dumb so we wouldn't suspect her. Very clever!

Only a kid who is gifted and talented could figure out complicated stuff like this.

"Miss Daisy," I said, "you're under arrest."

"What for?" she asked.

"For the murder of Ms. Todd!" I said.

Everybody in the class gasped.

"Are you out of your mind, A.J.?" said Miss Daisy. "Why would I murder Ms. Todd?"

"Because you thought she was going to take your job," I said.

"That's ridiculous, A.J.," said Miss Daisy.

"You've been playing dumb for too

long," I told her. "We're onto you. You're a murderer!"

"I am not!"

"Oh yeah?" I said. "It's funny how you walked in here just a few minutes after Ms. Todd ran out," I said. "You must have murdered Ms. Todd right in the parking lot!"

"I wasn't even in the parking lot!" said Miss Daisy. "I walked here."

"Tell it to the police," I said. "You lie like a rug. But we've got the goods on you. You're going to the slammer. Give me your hair. We've got to do a DNA test on it."

Miss Daisy sighed. "I need some bonbons."

Well, we never saw Ms. Todd again. Maybe she's dead or she went off to Antarctica to live with the penguins. Penguins are cool.

Maybe someday we'll find out if Ms. Todd was really a killer robot who was going to take over the world. Maybe somebody else will write that children's book about us. Maybe I'll think of a way to get kicked out of the gifted and talented program. Maybe someday we'll get somebody's hair and do a DNA test on it. Maybe someday I'll find out what DNA is. Maybe we'll sort out exactly who murdered who.

But it won't be easy!

Check out the My Weird School series!

#1: Miss Daisy Is Crazy!
Pb 0-06-050700-4

The first book in the hilarious series stars A.J., a second grader who hates school—and can't believe his teacher hates it too!

#2: Mr. Klutz Is Nuts!
Pb 0-06-050702-0

A.J. can't believe his crazy principal wants to climb to the top of the flagpole!

#3: Mrs. Roopy Is Loopy!
Pb 0-06-050704-7

The new librarian at A.J.'s weird school thinks she's George Washington one day and Little Bo Peep the next!

#4: Ms. Hannah Is Bananas!
Pb 0-06-050706-3

Ms. Hannah, the art teacher, wears clothes made from pot holders and collects trash. Worse than that, she's trying to make A.J. be partners with yucky Andrea!

#5: Miss Small Is off the Wall!
Pb 0-06-074518-5

Miss Small, the gym teacher, is teaching A.J.'s class to juggle scarves, balance feathers, and do everything but play sports!

#6: Mr. Hynde Is Out of His Mind!
Pb 0-06-074520-7

The music teacher, Mr. Hynde, raps, break-dances, and plays bongo drums on the principal's bald head! But does he have what it takes to be a real rock-and-roll star?

HarperTrophy®
An Imprint of HarperCollinsPublishers

www.dangutman.com